Milkyway

A horse and friendship story
By Kids for Kids

by
Aaliyah O. Ireson and Chloe J. Newenham-Kahindi

ACKNOWLEDGMENTS

Thanks to our editor Theodora O. Agyeman-Anane.We could never have made this book happen without you!

Milkyway

Cover Illustration: Aaliyah O. Ireson

Cover Sky Photos: Unsplash

Cover and Book Design: Theodora O. Agyeman-Anane

ISBN: 9798450608389

Text set in Times New Roman

Printed in North America

Book One

CHAPTER ONE

I positioned myself across the dining table, right in front of my mom, and said "I'm bored." Something that I had said five times already.

"Rachel, you can find something to do if you're bored, it's common sense." Mom answered, putting down the rolling pin she was using. "I can't help you."

"But Mom... there *is* nothing to do!" I said.

"There is a *lot* to do." She said. "You can do your chores. You can help your brother clean the stables."

"I don't want to help Josh." I said.

"How about you go see Joyce? You haven't seen her in a while." Mom suggested.

"Why can't she just call me if she wants to see me? She's always with Bella anyway!" I said, annoyed.

Joyce and Bella are both my friends. I met Bella at playgroups when we were four. She also has a horse, named Chariot, and he is a stallion. I was allowed to ride him for the first time the other day when I went over to Bella's house. I see him often, so I know him very well.

Joyce is a new friend of mine whom I met through Bella, but I don't see her often. We go to Horse Camp every year, but last year Bella went to a different Horse Camp and that's where she met Joyce.

"How about Coco? You still haven't ridden her." Mom reminded me.

Coco is my horse. When we moved onto our farm, Mom and Dad promised me a horse and I got Coco. I hadn't ridden her yet today, and it was pretty clear that Mom thought that Coco might be bored, too.

"Okay. I guess I will go for a ride." I sighed and begrudgingly went outside.

"Surprise!" a voice excitedly said as soon as I walked out of the door. It was Wendy, one of my very good friends, standing on my porch, her left hand on the door bell.

"I was just about to ring your bell," she said.

"Where is Slushy?" I asked her.

"I didn't bring my horse today." I'm always happy to see Slushy. She has a smooth white coat, thick mane, and a bushy tail. She is also fast. My family and I all think Wendy's horse is beautiful.

I've known Wendy for four years, since we met at Horse Camp. We've been good friends ever since. One thing I love about Wendy is how understanding she is. I'm always apologetic if I do or say something that's not very nice, but she seems to understand every time.

The last time I saw Wendy was the previous week at Horse Camp. We normally see each other in between camp days, but I hadn't had time to go to her house since then. She hadn't come over to me, either.

"Hi, Wendy. Sorry I haven't been available lately," I said, happy to see my friend.

"That's okay, I wouldn't have been available anyway."

"Why?" I asked.

"I had to ride Slushy everyday. She seems to be needing more exercise lately." Wendy answered.

"Oh, okay." I nodded.

"So," Wendy said as we made our way to the stables.

"How come *you* haven't been available?"

"Well, I went over to Bella's house the other day. I've been busy with Coco too. Sorry. I should've found time to come over to your house," I said apologetically.

"It's nice that you went to see Bella." Wendy said.

Bella and Joyce go to a separate Horse Camp from Wendy and I, that is why I see Wendy more often.

Also, I get along better with Wendy because we are both homeschooled and we both live on isolated farms. There isn't really anywhere for us to make friends, other than Horse Camp. Bella and Joyce go to the same school, they don't have any trouble making friends. Also, Bella seems to be closer to Joyce these days. We used to be best friends.

But now, that all seems to have changed.

Wendy and I can talk for hours. We tell each other everything and we enjoy talking about horses. We began talking about the latest TV series *The Mare*, a show about horses.

When I went home a few hours later, Mom asked me what I was able to do to entertain myself.

"Wendy was outside the house and we went for a walk to the stables… we took Coco for a ride." I said, and that was the end of it. Mom didn't press me for details, and I didn't give her any more information. We just went opposite ways.

Later in the day, Bella phoned. I was pretty nervous to start a conversation, because I wasn't used to talking to her on the phone.

"Hey Rachel!" she said, "I know you said you haven't seen Wendy for a while. Did you see her recently?"

"Yes, she came over earlier. How are you?"

"We're good. Joyce and I are going to Horse Camp now."

"Cool. Is Joyce with you?"

"No, but she's coming over in a few minutes. You know, Joyce is a really nice girl!"

I sighed. "Yeah. She's lovely."

"Right? I think she thinks the same thing about me." *Okay, that sounded just a little vain.* I thought. I didn't want Bella to phone me just to yak about Joyce, but I didn't say that. Instead I said "I have to go get Coco ready for her daily ride. Would you like to come over for a bit tomorrow?"

"Great, see you tomorrow." she said.

The following day, Bella and I took our horses for a ride. Being with Bella is different from being with Wendy, but still fun. Bella is more giddy and she has a good sense of humour. She is always trying to make me laugh, which is okay but can be kind of annoying.

We took Coco and Chariot for a ride. Coco is my favourite horse, but I also like Chariot.

"Shall we go back now? I'm getting tired!" I called out. Bella was a few feet behind me.

"Okay!" she called back.

Riding horses is like flying to me. When Coco gallops across the field, with my guidance, I feel like I have eagle's wings.

On the last Tuesday of Horse Camp, Eva, one of the girls at the camp came up to me and said "I wish you didn't spend so much time with Wendy." That comment hurt my feelings. I stared at her for a few seconds and then said, "Wow, Eva."

"What?" she said. "You spend so much time with Wendy now and you never spend time with me."

"You know that's not true, Eva," I said.

"Leave her alone, Eva, okay?" Wendy said, standing up for me. I appreciated that.

"I was just saying that I wish you treated me like a friend too," Eva said coldly.

"You are our friend, Eva," I said.

Eva shrugged her shoulders and walked off.

"That wasn't very nice," I said after Eva had left.

"Tell me about it," Wendy replied.

We don't take our horses to Horse Camp on Thursdays, so I'm always excited to see Coco after camp. On that last day of Horse Camp, Wendy and I rode our bikes to my house to see my horse. We were both exhausted, but we were really happy to go see Coco.

"Coco!" I cheerfully called out, walking into her stable. But something scared me.

Coco was gone.

CHAPTER TWO

*G*asping, I ran inside the house yelling:
"WHERE IS COCO?! WHAT HAPPENED?!"

"What? Isn't she in her stable?" Dad asked.

"She isn't!" I snapped. "I just went to her stable, and she is not there!"

"I'm sure I saw her recently. Are you sure she's not there?" Mom asked me.

"She's not there and I'm sure." I said rudely.

"Don't be rude to your mother Rachel." Dad said

"If you panic you definitely aren't going to find her, and you've got to calm down!" He put his hand on my shoulder.

"You just don't get it, do you? Coco is *my* horse, and *I'm* responsible for her! Who knows what could happen!" I shouted, tears still streaming down my face.

"Enough, Rachel," Mom said. "Whether Coco is your horse or not, you do not get to throw a tantrum like a two-year-old. Don't be rude to your father. Are we clear?"

"Yes," I grumbled.

"Good. Now go outside and look for her. Dinner will be ready in thirty minutes."

Wendy was still waiting for me outside.

"We have to go look for Coco, my parents don't know where she is." I said, tears streaming down my face.

"It's okay, we will find her." She told me.

"It's not okay," I said in panic. "We have to find her now! What could happen to her? Let's start by looking near the pond behind the stables. You take the right turn, I will go the opposite direction, and I hope we can find Coco along the way. I'll meet you midway. Do you have a watch?"

"Yes," Wendy said, "it's nearly five. I have to go home soon."

"Okay, can you go home after we look around the pond?" We continued on with our plan. I ran left, calling Coco. Wendy ran in the opposite direction doing the same.

We met midway.

"No luck." we said at the same time.

"Rachel?" I heard Mom calling me. "Dinner is ready."

"I have to go." Wendy said

"Well, you better go home now," I said with a heavy heart. We walked back to the stables. Wendy took her bike and cycled towards her house.

CHAPTER THREE

That evening I wanted to keep looking for Coco instead of going inside, but Mom made me come and join everyone for dinner. I ate my food quickly and I was out the door in no time.

"Coco," I called. I wanted to find Coco more than anything else. But something stopped me from moving. Maybe Coco will just find her way back home. I thought as I went through the fields around my farm. I was feeling so many emotions inside. On one hand I was mad at Coco, on the other I was mad at myself. *If only I had closed the stable door, none of this would have happened.* I thought.

I went back inside after thirty minutes, when I saw the farm night light coming on. "Why aren't you out looking for Coco?" Mom asked me.

"I don't want to find her." I lied.

"But you love Coco, what happened?" Mom said.

"Of course I want to find Coco," I sniffled. "I have looked everywhere I can think of but I can't find her."

"Try to rest tonight, you can go search for her tomorrow morning after breakfast." Mom said.

That night, going to sleep was difficult. I couldn't stop thinking about Coco. I sat on the edge of my bed, trying to figure out how she would have escaped. As I was still thinking about Coco, Josh came in.

"Hey, little sis," he said.

"Josh, not now. I have a lot on my mind."

"Okay, sorry," he said, shrugging and turning around to leave. "Mom wanted me to make sure you were okay. You know, you're kind of making too big a deal about the whole thing. I'm sure Coco is fine!"

"How do you know she's fine?" I asked.

"She has not been gone for long, Rachel. Nothing seriously bad can happen, not in five short hours."

"What if she *is* hurt?"

"That's what I'm saying, she wouldn't be. Not in five hours." Josh said.

"But, I want to go search for her *now*!"

"You can't. It's your bedtime."

"Ugh!" I grunted.

"What?" Josh asked.

"Did I say something?"

"Don't be rude to me. I'm your big brother!"

The rest of the week was all about searching for Coco. I hunted the whole farm. I didn't check the forest, but Coco had never been there before. There was no way she was there.

Wendy advised me to check wherever I thought Coco might be. I told her about what Josh said the night before, that I was making too big of a deal about it.

"A little advice: don't always listen to what your brother says!"

"He knows me better than any other kid," I said, "but he also knows how to annoy me."

"Exactly. Since he knows you so well, he probably knows just how to get to you, to make you react. Rachel, your horse is missing. I don't know how you're going to find her, but I'm pretty sure you're not going to find her if you just stare at the pond, waiting."

"First of all, Wisey…"

"Enough with the nicknames!"

"Okay. Well," I said, "I need to find Coco, right?"

"Right."

"Okay, so maybe I shouldn't stare at the pond, waiting as if she's going to come find me, but I've checked the whole farm. And I haven't found Coco." I complained.

"Who knows? Maybe she'll come back another day." Wendy said. I was starting to get annoyed at her too.

"This whole thing is making me more and more

worried, Wendy. Imagine if it was Slushy. What would you do?" I said, a hand on my hip.

"I would check the whole farm every day. I would call animal control. I would probably do all of those things, and I would just keep looking."

"Anything could have happened to her," I sighed.

"Keep looking!"

"But where?"

"Around the farm!" Wendy said impatiently.

"Okay, Wendy, you don't seem to understand. If I look all over my farm, and Coco isn't there, not even once, I don't have to keep looking in the same place where she isn't."

Coco needed food. She needed water. She needed me. I thought.

"Mom, can you phone the animal control?" I asked Mom that evening.

"I will consider doing that if you don't find Coco by the end of the month," she responded.

I cringed at the thought that maybe I wouldn't find Coco.

The following two weeks, I looked for Coco. I asked all the neighbouring farms if they had seen her.

Sometimes I went with Wendy. Bella, Joyce and even Eva decided to help post on telephone poles some photos of Coco I had printed. I made Josh help me once, but I knew I wouldn't be able to do it often.

"We have to call animal control," I said to Mom and Dad at dinner one evening after a busy day of searching.

"Before I do that," Mom said, "you need to check the whole farm. And that includes the forest behind it."

"Relax, Rachel," Dad said. "Coco is fine, I'm sure."

"But Dad, how can you be sure?" I asked. "Coco could be anywhere right now. I haven't been sleeping very well for the last two weeks. I've been so worried, searching everywhere..."

"Everywhere but the forest..." Josh interrupted me with a mean voice, clearly trying to scare me. "What's wrong, Rachel, are you scared?"

"Josh, that's enough. Maybe we should send *you* into the forest sometime!" Dad said.

"Your father is right," Mom said. "Enough, Josh."

"Okay, can we change the subject? The only conversation we've been having for the last two weeks is about Coco." Josh said, trying to exit the conversation.

I knew what Josh was doing. He was trying to

scare me. He was trying to prevent me from going into the forest.

I didn't understand it. *Why was Josh trying to prevent me from finding my horse?* I thought as I was getting ready for bed.

The following morning I woke up determined to find Coco, even if I had to go into the forest.

Soon after breakfast, I marched outside and stood on the front porch. In front of my eyes, I saw the field in front of the forest. Beyond that, I could see the dark green of the forest staring back at me.

CHAPTER FOUR

I was scared, but then I remembered the fact that Coco was lost. *She might be in the forest, more scared than me.* I thought.

I took a deep breath, gathering all the courage I could muster. I ran to the stables, and I grabbed my bicycle. I got on, and took another deep breath before pedaling fast towards the edge of the forest.

When I arrived at my destination, I got off and sighed. *This is going to be scary*, I thought.

I took another deep breath and I went into the forest.   Straight away, I saw one horse footprint after another.   I followed the trail and a few minutes later I saw a shadow.

"Coco!" I called. Hope returned.

I kept following the trail, until I got to a tree with brambles and blackberries surrounding it. Among the weeds and bushes, I saw something that made my day.

"Coco!" I yelled as I ran up to her. I was so happy to see her, I forgot about all the emotions that I had felt up to that moment. At the same time, I was sorry, too because I had basically let this whole thing happen.

Then I remembered that maybe she hadn't eaten in

almost two weeks, and she was probably starving. I tried to get her to stand up, but she was stuck.

"Hold on for a minute, okay?" I said to her, getting up. I ran back to my bike and zoomed back to my house.

"Hello?" I yelled, flinging open the door.

Dad came in holding a cup of coffee. "What's happened, Rachel?" he asked.

"Coco is stuck, and I need help to get her back," I said breathlessly.

"I can help," Dad offered.

Dad took me in his truck across the farm, and we went back into the forest. It was less scary, because I had him with me.

We rushed to Coco, and Dad helped me untangle her.

"Okay, she's probably hungry," I said to Dad as we guided her out of the forest. We took her back to the stable, and I gave her a lot of food and water. "I'm sorry, Coco," I said as I brushed her coat. "I'll make sure to keep your stable closed from now on. I promise." That was quite a promise to make to a horse, but I would make sure this wouldn't happen again.

Three weeks later, Coco began to struggle with

riding. Wendy and I both tried to figure out what in the world was wrong with her.

"Mom, can I give Coco a break from riding?" I asked her.

"Why does she need a break?" Mom asked.

"Because something seems to be wrong with her. She seems to want to rest a lot lately," I said.

"Okay, if she wants to rest, she should." Mom said.

I was glad that Coco could rest but I also wanted to know what was up with her. I didn't want Coco to work hard if something was hurting her. And I had a feeling that something was.

CHAPTER FIVE

*T*he next day, I went to check on Coco, and she seemed a little better but still tired so I decided to leave her to rest. I also noticed that her stomach was a bit bigger than usual, but I hadn't fed her yet. *Weird.* I thought as I walked out of her stable. *She is usually such a fit horse. What is wrong?*

Wendy came to visit me later that afternoon.

"How is Coco doing?" She asked. "How has she been doing since you found her?"

"She's tired all the time," I said, "and she looks different, somehow."

Wendy looked at Coco. "Bigger, somehow?" she asked. I nodded.

"Yes, look: her stomach is a bit bigger than usual."

"That's strange," Wendy said. "Have you been overfeeding her?"

"Nope. Not at all. Unless Josh is."

"Maybe she is not feeling well because she hasn't had good hay in the last three weeks." Wendy suggested.

"Maybe. I'll ask Josh."I went inside, and hunted the house for my big brother. "Josh!" I called.

He came in, holding a bag of chips.

"Wassup, little sis?" he said.

"Stop calling me little sis, Josh. I'm being serious this time," I said. Then lowing my voice I asked him: "Have you been overfeeding Coco?"

"No," Josh said. "And I'm telling you for real."

"Are you sure?" I said. "Coco might be sick."

Josh sighed. "At your age, little sis, you should know if your horse is sick. What do you go to a horse camp for?"

"Why do you keep calling me little sis?" I yelled at him. "Do you think I like it?!"

"I didn't say you did. The point is, keep track of your own horse, and get out of my face before I make you."

"Fine!" I roared. "I'll leave you alone, big bro!"

"He said he is not overfeeding her. That's at least what he says." I told Wendy once I got back outside.

"We need to figure it out. We can't just leave her hurting. Not if we can help it," Wendy said.

"Correct, we need to find out what is causing her to be tired all the time." I said.

"What did we learn at horse camp this summer?" Wendy asked.

"You're right. It's pathetic if we don't know how

to do this. We've been in a Horse Camp for four years now," I said.

"Okay, Rachel. What is wrong with a horse if it's always tired?" Wendy asked. "Is she doing too many exercises?"

"But she hasn't been jumping or running at all lately." I answered.

"What could be wrong with her?" Wendy asked.

Then it hit me.

"What if Coco is pregnant?" I gasped.

CHAPTER SIX

I ran back to the house "Mom!" I called, tears streaming down my face. I rushed in from the back door, crying unstoppably.

"Honey, what is wrong?!" Mom asked.

"It's Coco. I think she is pregnant." I wailed.

"Woah, woah! How did that happen?" Mom asked.

"And it really hurts her!" I wailed more. "I'm not sure, Mom! I don't even know that she *is* pregnant! I'm just guessing, but I'm pretty sure!"

"Okay, honey, I'm sure Coco is fine." Mom reassured me. "How did you get the idea that Coco is pregnant?"

I told her everything, as the story unfolded, it became more and more certain that my horse was *pregnant*. It didn't make sense. I mean, Coco? Pregnant? Then it all began to become clear.

Coco had gone missing about a month ago. Ever since then she's been struggling, and getting bigger and bigger by the day. That meant she must have mated with a male horse and got pregnant. But which male horse?

That meant that Coco had already been pregnant for at least two weeks before I found her in the forest because she mated. I was so mad at myself for not figuring it out earlier.

I took Mom outside to try and see what she thought. Coco seemed tired, but there was nothing we could do.

Mom said, "I'm sorry, honey. Coco is pregnant."

"You know that for sure?" I asked quietly.

"Honey, I can tell when people, and animals, are pregnant. I've pushed two babies out of me before."

And something told me I just had to accept that fact.

The following day, Bella came to visit me. We rode Chariot again, but I wasn't having fun. I could only think of Coco. As if Bella could read my mind she asked me "How's Coco?"

"Pregnant," I said.

"That is so exciting!" She let out a scream of joy.

"Exciting?" I rolled my eyes. "You don't understand!"

"Why is that bad? You are going to have another horse, Rachel!" she smiled.

"It hurts Coco!" I said "We don't know who she mated with."

"Of course it hurts her. That's what every woman has to go through if they get pregnant, Rachel. Can't you see?! It's not a bad thing!"

"It *is* a bad thing!" I roared.

Bella looked offended. "But, Rachel. You're going to have a foal. You're going to name it!"

"Well, that's not really something I can think of right now," I said coldly.

Just then, Bella pointed at someone in the distance.

"That's Joyce!" Bella said waving her free hand, "Over here!" She called her friend over. I knew Joyce was going to take Bella's side. This just infuriated me.

Joyce ran over. For some reason I felt jealous. All I wanted to do was to be at home at that moment. Nobody understood that Coco was not their horse, and of course they wouldn't care how much she is hurting. They would just be happy thinking about foal and names. Well, every-one except Wendy.

"Well, I gotta go," I said.

"Wait, hold up," Bella said. "Joyce! Rachel's horse is pregnant!!"

"Gggghhhh!" I roared. "Stop it! You didn't even ask my permission!" I knew right there and then that I would have to tell Wendy about this. Especially when Joyce said that she thought it was exciting too. Of course. Takin' Bella's side.

I went home with a dark cloud over my head. I felt

like I was fighting with the whole world. Wendy? Poof. She wasn't with me. But I was pretty sure that if she was, I would be mad at her too.

At home, Mom told me to check on Coco. But I was just sad. I hated the whole world at that moment. The day had turned out to be a bad bad bad one. And nobody was there to understand.

After quickly checking on Coco and helping Mom with dinner, I went up to my room with the phone. I wanted to talk to someone who understood my feelings.

CHAPTER SEVEN

Wendy was the one to pick up the phone after three rings. "Hey, Rachel," she said on the other side of the phone, "you okay?"

"NO," I said glumly. "I have bad news."

I noticed how the first thing she said was, "you okay?"

"What kind of bad news?" She asked. From the sound of her voice I could tell she was worried. I was worried sick that Bella and Joyce had told her about that afternoon. But she didn't say anything.

"Coco," I said. "She's pregnant, for sure!"

"Noooo!"

"I know. It kills me, too. I can't believe it." I said.

"Wow, Rachel. That must be sad. I'm sorry."

Something occurred to me that had never occurred to me before. Coco was going to give birth, and we needed to find someone who could deliver the foal. "I don't want Coco to have her foal yet," I said. "I'm still getting over her being pregnant."

"You know what 'pregnant' means, right?"

"Of course! *My horse* is pregnant."

"Right."

"What are we going to do when it's time for the foal to arrive?"

"Since my dad is a vet for big animals he can help with that," Wendy said. "Other than that, relax!"

I trusted Mr Walker, but I was still scared. I agreed to send Coco to his clinic for the remainder of her pregnancy.   Even though Wendy told me to relax, I couldn't.

I was pretty panicky for the rest of the remainder of Coco's pregnancy.

One day, ten months later, I went to Wendy's house to see if Coco was okay. When we went to the stables I found her lying on the floor. I wondered if she was ready.

"I think this is it," Wendy said. But she didn't seem as scared as I was. We had enough time to go and get fresh hay, and I stayed with Coco while Wendy went to get her dad. In the meantime, I called my own dad from my phone, to tell him that Coco was ready to give birth.

Wendy came back with her dad. Shortly after Dad and Mom came to the stables.

"I'm freaking out." I told them.

Wendy put her hand on my shoulder while my dad

pet Coco on her nose. I had never seen Coco struggle this way before. She moved very slowly.

"I need to go get everyone else," I said.

"There isn't enough time, Rachel!" Dad said annoyed. Then getting up he said "I will be outside if you need me."

We had to stay with Coco until the foal came. I cried a million tears as I whispered "Easy, girl."

We just waited. We waited for two hours, and when nothing was happening, I went outside to tell Dad.

It began to rain outside, so Wendy pulled the blinds. I
wanted to cry again, but stopped immediately. *If I cry, I won't be able to see properly, and I definitely want to be able to.* I thought. Soon, I saw Coco's stomach inflate and then shrink.

"I think she's having contractions now," Wendy said.

Soon, just when I thought the foal wasn't coming after all, I saw two tiny hoofs wrapped in what looked like white film. Quickly after that was the best part. The head of the foal started to peek through, and then the whole body followed.

Meanwhile, Coco was making no sound, but I could tell she was tired. She rested her head on the hay.

Coco did it! She was alive and the foal too. Tired, tired, but alive.

Coco glanced back at her foal, and then she stood up. The birth sac slid of the foal. When the foal saw Coco standing up, it tried to stand up too. Coco came closer to the foal, and as if she had said, *"you can do this"* the foal stood up.

"Good girl, Coco!" Wendy cheered. After a few minutes my friend pointed outside and said "Look. The storm has stopped!"

CHAPTER EIGHT

The foal turned out to be a boy. We wrote a list of possible names for him.

1. *Miracle, because it's a miracle that he's okay*
2. *Handsome, because he's so handsome*
3. *Milkyway, because his coat is grey with a rim of dark brown and a white mane*
4. *Storm, cause it was stormy outside when he was born*
5. *Precious, because he is precious*

We decided to go with Milkyway. He was the greatest gift we had ever received. We thought about Miracle, too, but we liked Milkyway. It really fit him with his dark brown rim and his white mane. There was no reason any of the other names wouldn't have worked. He *was* a miracle. He *was* handsome. It *was* stormy outside when he was born, and he *was* absolutely precious.

Wendy and I were the ones in charge of cleaning up. Privilege comes with responsibility, as my dad put it. Dad had phoned Josh to come over.

"I have to admit," Josh said, "he's cute."

My whole family thought Milkyway was beautiful.

Bella and Joyce came later to see him. They were more like our enemies now. They immediately wanted to know his name, and acted like he was theirs.

"Milkyway," we told them.

"Why didn't we get to help name him?" Joyce demanded.

"We were here when Coco delivered him," I reasoned.

"You saw Coco give birth?!" Bella yelled.

"Of course! I'm her owner!" I said, fed up with them.

"Wow, girls, I thought you were nicer," Joyce said.

"Who's going to keep him?" Bella asked, probably hoping to keep him herself.

"Well, *my* horse had him," I said quietly, not wanting to sound rude. "He'll need her."

"Leave her alone," Wendy said, standing up for me "Rachel should keep Milkyway. He's her horse."

"You really think Rachel should have him?" Bella snorted. "You know, *Miss Birthy*, Joyce and I could always share him."

"He is my horse because he's Coco's son, and Coco is my horse. Now, leave Wendy alone!" I said, standing up for Wendy this time.

Wendy looked at me, but I carried on. "You two

38

just turned on us suddenly. We never did anything to you."

"You did! You just do a bunch of things without us, like delivering Milkyway!" Bella yelled.

"Well, we're close friends," I said. "Leave us alone."

"Fine!" said Joyce, getting up. "You two are self-ish!"

"Well, my horse was the one who had him. It makes no sense just to give it away," I said.

"Right," Wendy said. "You're just being rude. We named him, and now you're acting like he was supposed to be yours all along." I caught Bella looking down at the floor, as if she was sorry. But she said something that changed my mind.

"You know what?" she said.

"What?" Wendy snapped.

"Enjoy your goo-covered horsie-pie," Bella said, running out of the stables followed by Joyce, laughing.

CHAPTER NINE

*T*hat night, I observed Coco strolling across the field, followed by Milkyway. She was still a bit slow, and I must say she was still quite wide.

As for Milkyway, he was very energetic but wobbly, even though he was just half a day old. His legs were long compared to his body, but he was really cute. I was happy for Coco, but I was also very tired. Wendy and I had been both worried and excited.

Usually, I would go to bed between eight and nine, but, today I went to bed at seven. I knew that was early for a twelve year old girl, but I was exhausted. I was pretty sure Wendy was really tired too. Though she hadn't said it, I knew she had been scared just as much as I was. I'm so grateful to have a friend like her who stands up for me. I was disappointed that Bella and Joyce had just turned on us for no apparent reason, but to be fair, I hadn't seen them in a while, and they probably were a little upset about that.

I fell asleep really quickly, maybe even five minutes after my head hit the pillow.

As Milkyway got older, he got bigger, stronger

and faster, but he was still quite young. I had to give him more and more attention as he grew. It seemed like Wendy had grown apart from me, though. I hadn't seen her for almost a month now. I wanted to think she had been off on summer holidays, but I saw from her Instagram page that she wasn't. I even texted her once and she didn't reply.

I went over to Wendy's house after I had done my daily math on Thursday. Mom had given me permission.

I rang the doorbell. Wendy's mom opened the door.

"Hi, Rachel," she said mannerly. "What brings you here today?"

"I'm here to ask if Wendy wants to come over."

"Wendy is out with Bella and Joyce."

After I had figured out what happened, I went to Eva's house. When Horse Camp ended I had become closer to her.

"Hi Rachel," she said, smiling.

"Eva," I said, "what's going on with the others?"

"The others? Is something wrong?"

"That's what *I'd* like to know," I said. "I haven't seen Wendy in almost a month. Bella and Joyce have kind of been unkind to us lately, but it's almost as if Wendy just turned from me and went to them."

"Sorry about that. Do you know where they are?"

"Not particularly," I said, "do you?"

"Well, I can only give you this: I saw the three of them walking by my house a few minutes ago. They were going toward Joyce's house."

"Thanks for letting me know," I said.

I ran three blocks to Joyce's house, and I rang the doorbell, red in the face. The person who came to the door was Joyce. Bella and Wendy were behind her.

"Hey, Rachel," Bella said cheerfully, as if nothing had happened. "What's going on?"

"I came here to ask *you* that," I said.

I caught Wendy's eye, and she looked away.

"Can I talk to Wendy for a second?" I said.

"Um, sure," Joyce said, turning to Wendy, "I think Rachel wants to talk to you."

As soon as Bella and Joyce were gone, I threw my hands out to my sides and let them fall back into position.

"Wendy, I think it's about time you told me the whole story. I thought you *hated* Bella and Joyce!"

"I don't *hate* anybody," Wendy said, "they came over to my house about a month ago and said sorry and since then we've been hanging out."

"Well, what about me?!" I yelled. "You've been

hanging out with these girls for almost a month, and you didn't come over to my house. Not even once. You didn't even reply when I texted you! And you know it, so don't give me that face!"

"What 'face'?" Wendy asked, looking guilty.

"The innocent face. You know very well that you haven't been very nice to me this month, and now it feels like all you want to do is be with people that hate me!"

"They don't hate you." Wendy defended them.

"I want to know what's up." I said rudely.

"Nothing's up," Wendy said quietly.

"Yeah, right," I said sarcastically.

I didn't say anything after that, but I let her speak.

"Look, Rachel. I've been hanging out with you ever since I met you at Horse Camp four years ago. Ever since then, I haven't said a word to them, except with you. I just wanted to hang out with them a bit. Alone."

"Okay," I said, "so why didn't you reply to my text?"

"Because you seemed like you were mad at me, Rachel!" Wendy yelled. "I wanted just a little space."

"Even Eva feels closer to me these days. It hurt me to see that you wanted to be Bella and Joyce's friend and not to come over to my house or even phone me or reply to my text."

"I'm sorry Rachel. I just thought I should have spent more time with them," Wendy said quietly. "You know, you're not my only friend in the world."

"I didn't say I was. But to think that you didn't come over for a month and didn't reply to my text…"

"I know. I'm sorry. I just…" Wendy started "they were upset for a reason, Rachel. But if you just get mad at them, they're never going to tell you how they feel."

"So," I said, changing the subject, "how's Slushy?"

"One second, Rachel. I need to tell you something."

"Yeah?"

"I think I know whose horse Coco had mated with." Wendy said as my heart sped up. Would I know how Coco got pregnant?

CHAPTER TEN

I ran home, feeling strangely happy.

"Mom!" I called, flinging open the door. Josh was sitting across from Mom on the kitchen counter. They were in the middle of a conversation.

"Hey, honey!" Mom said. "We have some big news!"

"I have news too," I said. "important."

"Yeah?"

"I know who Coco mated with!" I said.

"Who?" Josh asked.

"You know that wild horse I go to see once a week?" I said. "Coco mated with him!"

"REALLY?" Mom gasped.

"Uh-huh!" I nodded.

"Well, I have some big news to tell you, too."

"What?" I asked, my eyes wide. When Mom had big news to tell someone, it was usually something sad.

"Well," Mom said slowly, "somebody has offered to buy Milkyway."

"Who wants to buy him?" I asked. "He's not up for sale! We never put him up for sale!"

"Rachel, look. Horses are pets. You don't get to

keep a foal your horse has birthed for longer than six months." Mom said.

"How come some farmers have so many horses?" I asked. "You know what you're saying isn't true."

"They breed them, Rachel. Coco became pregnant by accident. We are not a horse breeding farm!" Mom said.

"Mom, please!" I begged. "You don't know how it feels to have someone tell you that they want your horse!"

"Rachel, look. I know how you feel, I really do. But, you'll still have Coco for as long as she lives. And, the truth is, you are going to find it hard to take care of two horses."

"Mom, he's my horse and I should get to choose whether I keep him or not."

"Okay. Listen. I will talk to the people who want him, and if they say it's okay for him to stay, he will stay. But, Rachel, if they say no, you have to be understanding. Okay?"

"Thanks, Mom, I appreciate it," I said, relieved.

"I'm going to phone them tomorrow, okay?"

"Alright Mom. That's fine."

That night I focused on the fact that Milkyway had

a chance of staying. I made a list of possible jobs I could get to earn some money to help if he stayed. I also prayed with my eyes squeezed shut that the people who wanted him would be understanding. Even if it meant I had to run through fire, I wanted Milkyway to be ours.

The following morning, I ran downstairs and poured myself a bowl of Cinnamon Toast Crunch, my favourite cereal. I was really eager to find out if Milkyway was staying or not. I ate my cereal as fast as I possibly could, but Josh told me to slow down. When breakfast was over, Mom phoned the people who wanted Milkyway.

"Mom?" I said as soon as she had hung up. She ate her breakfast, and I could tell she was stalling. When she didn't answer, I shook her shoulder, repeating, "Mom!"

"Honey, don't do that to me," Mom said.

"Tell me. Please," I begged. "Is Milkyway staying?"

"Okay, okay. Well, the people said that they would really really really like it if they could have Milkyway… however, they are moving soon, and they wouldn't be able to take him in now." Mom sighed.

"So?" I prodded.

"Well, they will call us back when they have moved, and they will see how they feel."

"So, what does that mean? Does that mean he can stay, at least for now?!" I asked hopeful.

"At least for now." Mom said carefully.

"What about, well, forever?" I said sweetly.

"It looks like they would really like to have him, but we'll have him for at least another five or six months."

"And then?" I was becoming a bit impatient.

"At the end of the last month, they will make their final decision. I don't know what that means, Rachel, but you did promise that you would be understanding, whatever they decide."

The next few months passed by quickly, but I wanted them to stay forever. I was scared. What if they liked him? I would know he was a good horse, but he would leave us forever. It felt like they were leaving him with us so I could feel sad while Milkyway was being so good. It was so sad. I wanted Milkyway to stay. It wasn't fair. He was my horse, and they were letting me have him, but just for now. The only hope I had was that they hadn't specifically said that he was leaving, but Mom had lately been telling me that it looked like he was going to be theirs. But, Mom had just made an assumption. He wasn't going, not for sure.

Sure, it looked likely. But I wasn't going to let my mind be fixed on that. I made a vow to myself: *I will let him go, if I have to let him go.*

ABOUT THE AUTHORS

Chloe Newenham-Kahindi has loved writing since she was three. This is her first published novel, but she has written many other stories. She is ten years old and lives in Victoria, BC, with her family and their pet dog Mango.

Her next project will be the *Mybig* series. Book One is coming out soon. She is very good friends with Aaliyah and has always loved animals.

Aaliyah Ireson is creative and loves to let her imagination flow. She spends most of her day drawing, reading books, writing stories and playing video games. Aaliyah loves dragons and other animals. She is very good friends with Chloe.

She is nine years old and lives in Saskatoon, SK, with her family and their rabbit Brownie.

Printed in Great Britain
by Amazon